Q: Just what is this "Princess Diaries, Volume IV and a Half"?

A: The number 4½ (aka IV and a Half) comes between the numbers 4 and 5, so this book comes between volumes 4 (IV) and 5 (V) of The Princess Diaries.

Q: When in Princess Mia's life does it take place?

A: In March, during her spring break from school. In other words, between books 4 (December–January) and 5 (April–May).

Q: Why is it being published?

A: Because we don't want you to miss a single sentence of Mia's diary entries!

BOOKS BY
MEG CABOT

MEG CABOT

The Princess Diaries, Volume IV and a Half

Project Princess

HarperTrophy®
An Imprint of HarperCollins Publishers

The author's proceeds from the sale of this book will be
donated to the Lower Eastside Girls Club of New York City
to help build their first ever permanent home.

Meg Cabot's proceeds from the sale of this book go to help build the first ever permanent home of the Lower Eastside Girls Club of New York City. This nonprofit community organization provides a range of innovative programming for girls and their families living in down-town Manhattan. The Girls Club's mission is: opening doors, empowering women, building community, girl by girl. To learn more about the Girls Club, their programs, and the building project go to www.girlsclub.org.

Harper Trophy® is a registered trademark of
HarperCollins Publishers Inc.

Project Princess
Copyright © 2003 by Meggin Cabot

Library of Congress Cataloging-in-Publication Data is available.

Typography by Alison Donalty
❖
First Harper Trophy edition, 2003
Visit us on the World Wide Web!
www.harperteen.com
10 11 12 13 OPM 10 9

Project
Princess

I am completely exhausted. I don't know why, when I must already bear the burden of having been born a princess—even though I was not aware of it until recently—that I also have been cursed with such a trying family.

I mean, it is bad enough that they waited until I was nearly fifteen before letting me in on the whole "oh-by-the-way-you're-a-princess" thing. But now they can't even agree on whether or not I can spend my Spring Break with the rest of the Albert Einstein High School Gifted and Talented class in West Virginia, volunteering for Housing for the Hopeful.

As if doing good works for the less fortunate was not what being a princess is all about!

And okay, I can see how my whole Princess-Di-and-the-landmines argument didn't work on Grandmère—who thinks I spend enough time in my overalls as it is—but my MOM? I just spent an hour impressing upon my mother Housing for the Hopeful's "theology of the hammer": how partnerships founded on common ground—for instance, a lot of people from different cultural, religious, and socioeconomic groups getting together to build a house—bridge theological differences by putting caring into action. I mentioned how everyone, no matter how uneducated, can use a hammer, turning it into an instrument that manifests peace and love.

My pregnant mom—who was lying on her bed watching *Stolen Women: Captured Hearts* on the Lifetime Movie Channel with a carton of Häagen-Dazs chocolate-chocolate-chip ice cream balanced on her enormous belly (even though she is supposed to be limiting her saturated fat intake to less than twenty grams daily due to her more-than-thirty-pound weight gain in the past half year)—just looked at me and asked, "Mia, are you in a cult?"

OH, MY GOD! Only the extreme hormonal imbalance my mother is going through right now could make her believe that my working to provide affordable housing for the poor so that they can live in dignity and safety is in any way comparable to religious fanaticism.

When I mentioned that out loud, however, my mother shrieked, "Frank! Come here, quick! Mia's in a cult!"

Thank God Mr. Gianini came into the bedroom—he'd been in the living room, practicing his drums—and explained to my mother in a calm, reasonable voice that Housing for the Hopeful is not a cult, that it is a nonprofit, nondenominational organization dedicated to eliminating substandard housing and homelessness worldwide. He also said that he himself had volunteered to escort students from Albert Einstein the past five Spring Breaks, and that the only reason he hadn't gone this year was on account of my mom being pregnant with his unborn child, the sex of which we do not know because my mom says if she knows it's a boy she won't have any incentive to push, men being the reason we even need organizations like Housing for the Hopeful. Because male politicians make such bad decisions when they are elected to public office, such as starting expensive and unnecessary wars before making sure all their constituents have decent housing first, etc.

So then I pointed out to my mom that Tina Hakim Baba, who isn't even *in* Gifted and Talented, and whose father owns a bunch of oil wells and is always worried about Tina getting kidnapped by some rival oil baron's henchmen, has been given special permission to go. And that Lilly Moscovitz, resident school genius and my best friend, is going. Ditto her boyfriend, Boris Pelkowski, violin virtuoso and mouth breather.

Then I added that my own boyfriend, Lilly's older brother Michael, is going, as well. I tried not to look too eager as I stressed this last piece of information. I mean, really, there's no reason to belabor the fact that Michael and I would be together, without parental supervision, in the wilds of West Virginia for five whole days. I was pretty sure my mom wouldn't be too thrilled if she realized this was the primary reason for my wanting to go. I tried to make it sound like the primary reason for my wanting to go was my desire to help those less fortunate than me.

Which is completely, 100 percent true. But also . . .

well, I sort of want to make out with my boyfriend without having his parents or my mother or stepfather or grandmother barge in on us.

I stressed to my mom that the trip is totally a school sanctioned outing, and would be fully supervised by Dr. Juan Gonzales, the director of the Northeast Division of Housing for the Hopeful; Albert Einstein High School's principal, Principal Gupta; Mrs. Hill from my Gifted and Talented class (not that I am gifted *or* talented, but whatever); Mademoiselle Klein from French; and Mr. Wheeton, the track coach and Health and Safety teacher.

Oh, and that—hello—the Appalachian Mountains are only, like, seven hours away from Manhattan by bus, and the whole trip is only for five days, so what is the BIG DEAL????

But my mom still looked a little skeptical . . .

. . . until I mentioned that Grandmère had declared that my wanting to go at all was entirely Mom's fault, for enrolling me in such a hippy-dippy school in the first place.

When I told Mom that, she got this *look* in her eye, and went, "Your grandmother said that? You know what, Mia? You can go. Now get out of the way, you're blocking Janine Turner."

It's a wonder I'm as well adjusted as I am, if you think about everything I have to put up with.

Well, whatever. After all that arguing, I'M GOING

TO WEST VIRGINIA!!!!!!!!!!! I must summon my last ounce of energy to tell my one true love of our impending bliss:

FtLouie: Michael! My mom said I can go!

LinuxRulz: Oh, hey, that's great.

Oh, hey, that's great? That's IT? This is the full extent of Michael's appreciation for all my hard work and whining? *Oh, hey, that's great?*

Maybe it just hasn't sunk in yet.

FtLouie: To West Virginia! Where we will be alone AT LAST!

LinuxRulz: Well, not really. Because everybody else in G and T is going to be there, too.

Oh, my God. This is going to be harder than I thought. Michael is obviously not thinking along the same lines I am concerning this trip. He is probably looking forward to doing some good for the less fortunate. Which I am too, of course.

But I am also looking forward to making out with my boyfriend under the West Virginia stars. . . .

Must work on planting seed of romance in him, so it can come to fruition in time for major make-out session in our nation's thirty-fifth state!!!!!!!!!

5

Lilly is so excited about the West Virginia trip, she can't talk about anything else. But she is excited for a different reason than I am. She is bringing her video camera, and she is going to tape the trip and show it later on her public access cable television program, *Lilly Tells It Like It Is*. She says it is going to be a searing commentary on the inadequacies of our public housing system.

"You should write something about it, Mia," Lilly just said to me. "You know, something allegorical, like about how building a house compares to building an analytic framework for government policy of a small European principality like Genovia. I bet anything they'd put it in the school paper."

But really Lilly was just rubbing it in that, ever since I discovered that my only talent is that I can write things in a semi-entertaining manner and joined the school paper, *The Atom*, all the editor has let me write is the weekly cafeteria menu, since I'm a freshman and I haven't Paid My Dues.

But even if I *could* get Leslie Cho to print my story, it's not like I actually *know* anything about building houses. It's not like I am going to be able to contribute anything to the Albert Einstein High School student construction team, considering what a talentless freak I am—except maybe for the whole writing thing. But what good, under circumstances such as these, is being able to *write*? It would be so much cooler if I were skilled at using a lathe, or something actually *useful* to society.

Maybe I should just face the fact that the only thing I can do moderately well is write, and possibly order Chinese food, and that it is highly unlikely that I have some kind of hidden talent for hanging drywall and that I am going to discover it while building houses for the homeless over Spring Break.

Although—I am sorry—but if I were a poor person, I would so rather have me than Boris Pelkowski build my house. Even if the alternative was *no* house, I would not want Boris building my house. I know Boris is the most gifted person in our whole Gifted and Talented class, but once during a school orchestra concert Boris went into the third-floor stairwell so he could practice his solo in private and he ended up locking himself out and had to bang on the steel doors for hours before anyone found him. I mean, the concert had already ended by then, and everybody had gone home. It was lucky the custodian was still on duty or Boris might have been trapped in that stairwell all weekend. Without food or water, he might have died, and on Monday when everybody came back to school, all they'd have found was this skeleton clutching a violin and wearing a sweater tucked into its pants.

But that's just my opinion.

Friday, March 11,
Lunch meeting of the Albert Einstein High
School Housing for the Hopeful Brigade

I am starting to have grave reservations about West Virginia, and not just because Michael hasn't once asked me if I am planning on bringing my cherry ChapStick (his favorite flavor). I mean, I know there are poor people there and all, but it is still in AMERICA, for crying out loud.

But Dr. Gonzales just gave us this list of things we need to bring with us, and Lilly and Michael and Boris and Tina and I are just sitting here, reading it, going, Hello, is this a joke? Like, what is a five-gallon solar shower bag? Where would you even buy one of those? And what is with the potassium-rich, non-melting snack items? What are THOSE? What are we going to need potassium for? Don't they have grocery stores in West Virginia? I mean, can't we just go to the deli and buy a banana?

Other things we are supposed to bring include:

Tool belts or cloth nail pouch
Hammer with claw
Gloves for handling rough lumber, hammers, shovels,
    etc.
25- to 30-foot tape measure
Utility knife

Wire cutter and/or tin snips to cut bailing and chicken
  wire
Small nail puller or cat's claw
Carpenter's pencil
Small square: combo, tri, or carpenter's
Small (short shank), sharp handsaw
Plumb line (optional)

Um, hello. I am a princess. I don't have any of these things. Need a scepter? I'm your girl. Nail puller? Not so much.

And hello, you would think they would give us some lessons on, like, gypsum board or whatever, but no. Instead, Dr. Gonzales just gave us these release forms that our parents are supposed to sign, saying that they won't hold Housing for the Hopeful responsible in the event that we are maimed or killed on the trip.

Maimed or killed!!!!!

Tina Hakim Baba just raised her hand and wanted to know why the handout says we need to bring a week's supply of wet wipes with us. Dr. Gonzales says because on cloudy days our five-gallon solar shower bags might not warm up enough and so we should be prepared either to take a cold shower or use wet wipes to clean ourselves.

Um, excuse me, but do wet wipes even work on b.o.? How am I going to make out with my boyfriend if I SMELL????

I *really* started panicking when Dr. Gonzales asked us all to turn to page 2 of the handout. That's because page 2 said:

- Drink plenty of sports drinks, Gatorade, or cranberry juice the week prior to departing. Drink the Gatorade provided to you at the worksite to raise your electrolyte and potassium levels.

- There are a great many flying insects in this climate. You will need insect repellant.

- Don't pet the local animals since they often carry diseases. Wash your hands immediately if you do.

- Don't drink the shower water or water from the local spigots.

Don't drink the water or pet the animals? Insect repellant? Gatorade?

Oh, my God, what have I gotten myself into??????

Grandmère can't believe Mom is letting me go to West Virginia. She says she doesn't know who's crazier, Mom for letting me go, or me for wanting to go in the first place. She read over the release forms and told me she hoped I'd have fun in boot camp.

"It's not boot camp, Grandmère," I told her. "It's a nonprofit, nondenominational organization dedicated to eliminating substandard housing and homelessness worldwide."

"Then why," Grandmère wanted to know, "does it say here that you will need to rise every morning at six A.M.?"

"Because," I said, snatching the forms back from her, "that's probably when they serve breakfast."

Grandmère shook her head. "The last time I got up at six A.M. was when the Germans were shelling the palace, back during the war. Nothing short of anti-aircraft fire should get a princess out of bed before eight. Anything earlier is indecent. It is not too late, Amelia, for you to join me in Palm Springs, where I am going to relax from the stress of our daily princess lessons. It isn't easy, you know, teaching a young girl all she needs to be regent, day in, day out. Are you sure you don't want to come with me? There's no need to wear insect repellant in the desert. And there won't be any wet wipes. Just the beautiful crystal waters of the hotel pool, and Belgian waffles from room service . . ."

"No!" I yelled, because the waffle part sounded really tempting. I bet nobody at the spa where Grandmère is going has to worry about their potassium level. "I am going to spend my Spring Break doing something good for mankind." And, hopefully, making out with my boyfriend. Oh, yes, and discovering that I am a skilled shingle layer. Hey, you never know. "Remember Prince William? He spent a YEAR after high school in Chile helping the poor. I'm just going to West Virginia, and only for five days. I think I can hold out for five days of getting up at six A.M."

Grandmère just took a sip of her sidecar and petted Rommel, her semi-bald toy poodle.

"Suit yourself," she said. "But I hope this doesn't mean you are going to start going about in native wear, like those bulky Chilean sweaters Prince William started wearing. You know how wool gives you a rash."

I told Grandmère they don't wear sweaters in West Virginia, and she asked what they do wear, then, and I had to admit I didn't know. That's when she stabbed a finger at me and went, "Ah ha! I'll tell you what they wear in West Virginia! Gunnysacks! That's what they wear in West Virginia!"

I told Grandmère that contrary to what she might believe, the Depression is over and nobody wears gunnysacks anymore.

But I don't know. I mean, what about that movie *Nell*, starring Jodie Foster, where she played that deaf mute who lived way out in the woods and was always going on about "dancin' een the weend"? I am pretty sure that was set in West Virginia. Or one of the Carolinas. Close enough. And she was wearing a gunny-sack. Or a housedress at the very least.

Oh, my God, I hope they don't expect us to dress like the natives in order to blend in! I don't own a housedress! I don't even think you can buy one of those in New York!

Friday, March 11, 11 p.m., the loft

I was so worked up about all the gunny-sacks and Gatorade that when I got home I asked Mr. Gianini if there was something he maybe wasn't telling me about his past trips with Housing for the Hopeful. Mr. G has never actually been to West Virginia before, but he went to Mexico and some Texas border towns with H for the H. He went, "Really, Mia, I can't say enough positive things about the experience. It really taught me to appreciate all that I have."

Which is fine, but didn't really answer my question about the gunnysacks. He did say I could borrow his hammer, though.

So I went online and instant messaged Michael, because after all, he is my heart's desire, and the only person on earth who can soothe me when my soul turns fractious as an injured pony.

But even though he is my reason for living and all of that, Michael was totally unhelpful about the whole gunnysack thing.

LinuxRulz: Mia, the people we are going to build homes for are poor, not demented. I am sure they are going to be wearing something other than bags. I mean, it's not going to be like in *Deliverance*.

I have never seen *Deliverance* because I don't like movies where things jump out at people from behind trees, but I pretended like I had, because I want Michael to think I am mature for my age. After all, he is a senior and I am only a freshman. I have to do what I can to keep him from remembering I am only fourteen and three quarter years old.

FtLouie: I know. But I mean, did you ever read *Christy*?

This is kind of a stupid question to ask a guy, since the only guy I know who has read *Christy* is my neighbor Ronnie, who is now a girl. But whatever. Michael is way well read, for a member of what my mom likes to call the cult of patriarchy.

FtLouie: Because *Christy* takes place in the Smokey Mountains, which are practically the same as the Appalachians, and everybody in it gets typhoid because of the unsanitary conditions, including Christy, and I am just saying, maybe that's why we're not supposed to touch the animals. . . .

LinuxRulz: Mia, stop worrying so much. If it were really unsafe, do you think Principal Gupta would be going?

FTLOUIE: Principal Gupta does some very strange things sometimes. Remember when she agreed to play Officer Krupke in the drama club's production of *West Side Story*?

LINUXRULZ: Mia, instead of obsessing over the possibility of contracting typhoid and/or having to wear a gunny-sack, why don't you try to keep in mind the most important aspect of this whole trip?

I thought maybe he meant the fact that we were going to get to make out beneath the West Virginia stars. But since that seemed unlikely, given our last few conversations, I decided he must mean the whole thing where I might possibly find out that I am good at something besides recording every single last detail of my existence in this diary, which is not exactly a worthwhile skill.

But then I realized he couldn't possibly mean that, because I hadn't mentioned my secret fantasy that it turns out I am an excellent plasterer, or whatever. So instead I wrote:

FTLOUIE: You mean the part where we are helping the poor to self-actualize?

LINUXRULZ: No, I mean the part where you and I get to

spend five whole days together without any interference from your grandmother.

Ooooh! So he *is* catching on, after all!!!

Michael's right. Who cares about typhoid when there's *kissing*?

Well, the kissing hasn't started yet.

That's because before we'd even gotten to the Lincoln Tunnel, Boris got carsick and had to throw up in a paper bag, and Lilly said no way was she sitting by him anymore, and told Michael to move so she could sit by me, and when Michael said no, Boris threw up some more, only this time he missed the paper bag, and it went all over the floor, and Principal Gupta and Mrs. Hill had to clean it up, but they didn't do a very good job on account of not having any paper towels or anything, so we all had to move to the back of the bus, away from the vomit fumes, and Michael was the only one who volunteered to stay with Boris and make sure that next time he threw up in the bag.

My boyfriend is so cool. Not only is he incredibly smart and a very talented musician and skilled with computers and an excellent kisser and all of that, but he is also extremely compassionate. Maybe he will be a doctor someday, and discover a cure for cancer. I certainly hope so, because that's the only way the Genovian Parliament is going to approve me marrying him.

I am not worried, though. Michael is a man among men, and will doubtlessly do something extraordinary with his life that will win the hearts of the Genovian people, just as he has won mine. If only I had as many useful talents as Michael does. It would be nice if I could play the guitar *and* knew html.

Anyway, even though I offered to sit up in the front of the bus with Michael and help him pass paper bags to Boris, he said, just like Daniel Day-Lewis in *The Last of the Mohicans*, "No, Mia, save yourself," so now Lilly, Tina, and I are all crammed into one seat until we get to the first rest stop on the N.J. Turnpike and the bus driver can give the floor a good hosing. Principal Gupta says as soon as we pull over, she is going to buy some Dramamine and make Boris take it. Boris says Dramamine makes him drowsy and robs him of his personality.

I can't wait.

Anyway, Lilly has already started filming. She got a very good closeup of the vomit. She started filming at five A.M., which is the time everybody had to be at Albert Einstein High School with all of our stuff in order to catch the bus. Everybody had a lot of stuff, especially considering that this trip will only last five days.

The person with the least luggage is Lars. Even though I lobbied very hard not to be accompanied on this trip by my royal bodyguard, my dad insisted. He said he wasn't thrilled about my going in the first place—Dad wants me to spend every vacation I get in Genovia—but since Mom had already said I could, he wouldn't contradict her. He wouldn't, however, allow me to go without protection from would-be kidnappers. All of my arguing that Tina was getting to go *sans* personal security system—Mr. Hakim Baba has no enemies, it turns out, in West Virginia, and so Wahim gets a well-earned vacation . . . only he's not as happy about it as you would think, since it means Lars gets Mademoiselle Klein all to himself . . . well, and Mr. Wheeton—seemed to fall on deaf ears. Lars was going, my dad said, and that's it.

At least Lars travels light. All he brought is one small duffel bag. I asked Lars where his sleeping bag and pillow were, and he just smiled. I hope he does not think he is sharing mine. I love my bodyguard, but not that much.

Anyway, Lilly is filming everything on the bus so we won't forget a thing. She took a good long shot of the sign hanging over the bus driver's head. The sign says:

I AM YOUR BUS DRIVER, <u>CHARLIE</u>.
SAFE, COURTEOUS, AND RELIABLE.
PLEASE STAY BEHIND THE YELLOW LINE.

While we were stuck in traffic in front of the Lincoln Tunnel, Lilly asked us what we thought Charlie would do if Principal Gupta suddenly threw herself across the yellow line.

"Because Charlie is safe and reliable," Tina said,

"he would probably go, 'Miss! Stay behind the yellow line!'"

"Yes," I agreed. "But because he is also courteous, he'd probably put it like, 'Please, miss! Stay behind the yellow line! Thank you!'"

For some reason, this made us laugh until we felt like throwing up ourselves.

Only six and a half more hours to go until we get there.

Michael and I are finally sitting together, but we are not making out yet, because Michael does not believe in public displays of affection, because, as he says, Some Things Are Private.

Which I fully understand and appreciate. I mean, it is not like I want him to go around Frenching me in the caf, or whatever.

But you know, *holding hands* wouldn't hurt.

On the other hand, it is sort of uncomfortable to hold hands for any extended period of time. Mine always starts getting all sweaty. My hand, I mean. Michael's doesn't. His hands are never sweaty. Maybe on account of him being a musician and all.

Maybe I am suffering from a genetic mutation. I mean, on top of my flat-chestedness and lack-of-useful-skill-ism. Maybe I've got an extra-sweaty-hand chromosome, or something.

Anyway, Charlie, being safe, courteous, and reliable, hosed down Boris's barf when we got to the Molly Pitcher Service Area, and then we all got back on board, and with the windows down, you really can't smell it that much. Principal Gupta gave Boris a good dose of Dramamine, and now he is unconscious with his head lolling against Lilly's shoulder. I guess he wasn't kidding about motion-sickness medicine causing

22

him to lose his personality. We should give him some every day, if you ask me.

Still, even though Boris spent most of the beginning of the trip barfing, that hasn't stopped him and Lilly from being the first couple to get caught making out. They were first spotted sucking face in the Roy Rogers at the rest stop, and a sharp rebuke from Principal Gupta caused them to spring apart.

But just recently I looked toward the back of the bus, and they were at it again! Those two can't keep their hands off each other!!!

I wish Michael would look back there, and realize maybe a *little* PDA couldn't hurt. . . .

Oh, my God, I am so tired. And my hair smells a little like Boris's barf. I can't wait until we get there, and I can wash my hair, and then all the kissing can start.

Oh . . . my . . . God.

We're here. We finally arrived. We finally arrived, and Charlie unloaded our bags, and then we had to pick them up and carry them to . . .

OUR TENTS!!!!!!!!!!!

YES!!!!!!!!!!!!!!!! TENTS!!!!!!!!!! WE ARE SUPPOSED TO STAY IN TENTS!!!!!!!!!!

I realized, of course, that we'd be sleeping in tents. I saw pictures of them in the brochure.

But the tents in the brochure had, like, wooden floors, and were raised off the ground. These tents have no wood supports at all. And they are RIGHT ON THE GROUND. WHERE THERE ARE ALSO SNAKES.

I have never slept in a tent in my life. Seriously, I am not trying to be a princess about this, but, I mean, what about bears? And don't tell me there are no bears around here, because we are SURROUNDED by woods, there is NOTHING but woods in West Virginia, and yeah, Principal Gupta keeps going on about how beautiful it is, and look at the mountains and smell the clean, fresh air, but hello???? BEARS!!!!!!!!

And didn't she ever see *The Blair Witch Project*? I mean, I will admit I watched that entire movie with my eyes closed, but it SOUNDED really scary, and I believe it took place, um, where? OH YES, THE WOODS!!!!!!!!!!

This is it. We are all so dead.

Lars says not to worry, that he will make sure no wild animals or serial killers get into the tent Lilly and Tina and I are sharing. But I don't know. That's what the people in *The Blair Witch Project* did, and look what happened to them! All they found of that one guy was his finger! I do not want to find Lars's finger! I do not want to lose Lars, he is an excellent bodyguard with a good sense of humor. Plus he doesn't mind when Michael and I make out. Do you know how rare that is in a bodyguard????

Anyway, West Virginia itself isn't so bad. So far we haven't met one person wearing a gunnysack or playing the banjo in a menacing way. Everybody looks . . . well, just like people in New York. We haven't met our "host family" yet. The way it works is, we are all split into groups, and then each group is assigned to a host family, and then they work on that family's house. I was very scared about the group thing, like, that I might get assigned to a group away from all my friends, where I wouldn't know anybody. But fortunately, you get to pick your own group. So Michael, Lilly, Boris, Tina, Mrs. Hill, Lars, me, Dr. Gonzales, and this one boy, Peter Tsu, who is a junior and is on the wrestling team, are all in one group.

I feel kind of sorry for our host family, to tell you

the truth. Because I mean, except for Dr. Gonzales and possibly Peter Tsu—who I don't know anything about—none of us has ever built anything before. Some of us have never even held a hammer before.

Our host family's house has a fair chance of ending up looking like complete crap.

Oh, God, there's the bell. We are supposed to gather in the "dining tent" now for orientation and supper. I am having grave reservations about all of this. I mean, besides the tents and the whole thing where we are probably going to end up ruining our host family's chances of getting decent housing, there is the fact that they have separated the girls' tents from the boys' tents—which is going to make it VERY difficult to find a place private enough to suit Michael's sensibilities for any make-out session that might lie in our future—with—I shudder to write it—Port-O-Lets!

Yes!!!!! That is right!!!!!! There are not even any working indoor toilets—at least until we install our host family's. We have to use Port-O-Lets!

And don't even get me started on the whole shower thing. The need for solar shower bags came into startling clarity when I saw the shower area, which is just a bunch of tarped-off stalls with hooks to hang your shower bag from.

It looks like it's going to be wet wipes the whole way, as it is drizzling steadily and there is not a hint of sun.

And you can't wash the smell of barf out of your

hair with wet wipes. Believe me, I tried.

The bell again. Got to go. Must find a place to hide this journal so the bears/serial killers/Blair Witch won't find it while I am gone.

I really should try to get used to all this, because if I ever want to volunteer with Greenpeace and help save the whales, the living conditions could be even worse.

Saturday, March 12, 9 p.m., Hominy Knob, West Virginia

We met our host family. They are Angie and Todd Harmeyer and their two children, three-year-old Mitchell and two-year-old Stefano. I swear that is the baby's name. Stefano. There is another baby on the way, too. Mrs. Harmeyer is due in a month, though if you ask me, she looks like she could blow at any moment.

Mrs. Harmeyer has a job sweeping up hair at a beauty salon in downtown Hominy Knob, which consists of a grocery store, a credit union, a hardware store, a consignment shop, and the beauty salon. Mr. Harmeyer has been unemployed since the local tire factory burned down. Both Mr. and Mrs. Harmeyer are very excited about their new house. They have been living in a trailer since they got married. Mitchell is especially excited about the prospect of having his own room. Right now, he has to sleep in the same bed as his mom and dad.

After we met the Harmeyers, and we were all standing in line to get our dinner—salad, corn on the cob, sloppy joes (being a vegetarian, I just took a bun and some of the vegetables), string beans, and cherry cobbler, for dessert—Mrs. Harmeyer asked me if it was true about my being a princess and the tall guy behind me being my bodyguard, and I said it was true.

"Well, whatcha doin' spendin' your Spring Break around here, then, if you're a princess?" Mrs. Harmeyer wanted to know. "If I were a princess, I'd spend my Spring Break in Cabo San Lucas, ridin' on one of them jet skis."

I explained to Mrs. Harmeyer that I had been compelled to join Housing for the Hopeful instead of spending my Spring Break riding on jet skis out of a keen sense of civic duty and a desire to learn new skills.

Mrs. Harmeyer just looked at me funny and went, "What?"

So then I told Mrs. Harmeyer I was there to make out with my boyfriend. She looked really interested then and wanted to know which of the guys in line was mine, and when I pointed to Michael she went, "Ooooeeee, he's a looker," which filled me with internal pride but also made me feel like smacking her.

So then I thought I had better change the subject, and asked Mrs. Harmeyer if she knew the sex of her unborn child yet. Mrs. Harmeyer surprised me by saying she didn't want to know, since if it was another boy, she knew she'd never push.

I was shocked to hear a woman in West Virginia echoing the exact same thing my mom back in New York City is always saying, and I asked Mrs. Harmeyer if she, like my mom, was an opponent to the cult of the patriarchy, to which Mrs. Harmeyer replied, "Gosh, no, I just want somebody I can buy Barbies for, instead of G. I. Joes."

After informing Mrs. Harmeyer that I fully understood her feelings, I took my food and went and sat down by Michael. Lilly was at our table, too, filming everyone. She filmed all the Hominy Knob locals who filed curiously past our table, pausing occasionally to ask me where my tiara was (answer: "Back in New York"), what it felt like to be a princess ("Okay") and why on earth I'd come to Hominy Knob ("To achieve self-actualization through selflessly helping others"). I didn't think the locals—aside from Mrs. Harmeyer—would appreciate hearing about my desire to suck face with my boyfriend.

After dinner, Lilly declared she had enough footage for a miniseries, let alone a single episode of her show. She decided she was going to have to do a month-long tribute to Hominy Knob on her cable access show. She decided to call the documentary "Sour Mash and Medicaid: The Failure of the Federal Government to Ease the Burden of the Rural Poor."

It will, she says, bring the current administration to its knees.

After dinner, Dr. Gonzales talked for a while, but I didn't pay much attention because I was thinking about the Port-O-Lets. Now I know why we'd been instructed to bring flashlights. There are no lights in the Port-O-Lets, so if you have to go in the middle of the night, you have to use your flashlight to see by. What's more, there's no telling what else might be sharing that

Port-O-Let with you. I mean, if you ask me, it's the perfect hangout for spiders, possibly black widow spiders, whose bite can be deadly. At least according to the Discovery Channel.

I am definitely bringing my insect repellant with me to the bathroom every time I have to go.

It was after Dr. Gonzales's long, boring talk that things really started to look up. That's because, walking back to our tents, Michael took my hand (it was dark out, so no one saw), then pulled me behind a tree and started kissing me in a highly romantic manner. It definitely took my mind off the Port-O-Lets for a little while. Good thing I had my cherry ChapStick handy.

But then Michael was like, "What's that smell?" and I sniffed and realized he was talking about my hair, which *still* smelled like Boris's barf.

Why didn't I bring any Febreze with me? WHY?

Anyway, the barf smell kind of ruined the mood. Besides, you couldn't even see any stars, it was drizzling so much.

Oh, no. The "lights out" bell. We have to turn out our flashlights now, and go to sleep. I don't know how anyone can be expected to sleep out here in the wilderness. There are all sorts of weird noises, like hooting owls and crickets and stuff. At least we don't have to worry about bears, though. Lars opened his duffel bag and pulled out a pup tent, complete with an inflatable air mattress, and set it up right in front of our door.

While this will make going to the Port-O-Let in the middle of the night slightly difficult—and will also, sadly, discourage any nocturnal visitations from boys— it makes me happy to know that Lars is out there with his Glock 9 mm and his nunchaks . . . even if he, like the rest of us, can't sleep due to the incredibly noisy owls.

I miss Manhattan already. What I wouldn't give to be lulled to sleep by the dulcet tones of a car alarm.

Sunday, March 13, Noon, the dining tent

Oh, my God, every inch of me is sore. It is no joke trying to sleep on the ground. And the sides of our tent kept flapping all night, and I thought it was the Blair Witch trying to get in.

Plus when we woke up, everything was drenched with dew. DEW. There is no dew in New York City. Pigeons, maybe. Lots of rats. But no dew.

Dew is my new enemy. Although thanks to it, my hair no longer smells like Boris's barf. Now it just smells like . . . dew.

It doesn't help that all I've done all morning is hold up wood frames. Apparently I am hopeless at hammering, sawing, drilling, *and* pouring cement. Good thing I came all the way to West Virginia to find that out.

So I was in charge of holding up the wood frames while other people hammered them in, a task that requires no skill whatsoever, just plenty of upper body strength . . . which I am, of course, lacking, but I am not about to admit it to anyone. At least, not out loud.

Still, those frames are HEAVY! I mean, building houses is not easy.

Thank God for Michael, Lars, Dr. Gonzales, and Peter Tsu. I don't mean to be sexist, but at this point in the building stage, the guys are definitely doing a better job than the girls—although Tina has proven to be pretty adept with the nail gun (lucky duck). I am pretty sure she is just doing it to look good in front of Peter Tsu, who has surprisingly shapely forearms—as Lilly was quick to point out and film for posterity. Peter is almost as hot as Mulan's boyfriend, and he has the added bonus of not being a cartoon character.

Nobody could be hotter than my boyfriend, though. I just wish it were sunnier out so Michael would get all sweaty and have to take his shirt off. That would make building a house WAY fun.

Well, that and actually knowing I was contributing to its construction in some meaningful way.

Anyway, our house is going up more quickly than anyone else's, despite our great handicap: Boris. While I am in no real way *helping* to build our house, at least I am not making things worse, the way Boris is. So far he has had two asthma attacks thanks to all the sawdust, and dropped a cinderblock on his foot (it will be all right, it is just bruised, Dr. Gonzales says). We have now assigned him to keeping Mitchell and Stefano from wandering too close to the chain saw, and refilling everybody's Gatorade containers.

Oh, yeah. I know why the Gatorade is so important now. Building a house is VERY tiring. You have to replace your electrolytes constantly.

Mr. Harmeyer says beer is better for replacing electrolytes than Gatorade, but Dr. Gonzales pointed out to him that alcohol dehydrates the body very quickly, and after that, Mr. Harmeyer shut up.

Lilly, who has been filming our progress with the framework of the house, insists that this new documentary is going to rival her most celebrated work of all, "Travels With Lana's Coccyx Bone" (which Lilly shot, using somewhat crude animation, after Lana Weinberger's coccyx bone broke off and disappeared into her bloodstream, thanks to a fall from a badly spotted basket toss. "Travels" showed Lana's coccyx bone moving through Lana's body, carrying a little suitcase and visiting with the other bones and stuff).

Lunch is salad, cornbread, mashed potatoes, and pork tenderloin sandwiches. I am just having salad and mashed potatoes. I am sick of corn already, though I understand that it is a staple of the West Virginia diet, like bagels and lox are in New York.

Sunday, March 13, 9 p.m., the tent

Too tired to give full account of day. Just held up more wood frames. For hours.

Dinner: salad, Tater Tots, hamburgers, corn. Just ate salad and Tater Tots. Sight of corn makes me want to puke.

Fell asleep during inspirational speech by Dr. Gonzales. Woke up with head on Michael's shoulder. He was very nice about it. Hope I didn't drool.

Can't believe I am too tired even to make out with own boyfriend.

Am going to sleep right now, too exhausted to wait for lights out.

Monday, March 14, Noon, the dining tent

Woke to full-on rain. Wet wipes instead of showers for everyone. That's okay, my muscles would have been too sore to carry my five-gallon solar shower bag to shower area anyway. Besides, I'm freezing—the dew soaked through my sleeping bag, right down to my pajamas. I feel like I've already had a shower.

Fortunately we had already framed in the roof of the Harmeyers' house. Spent morning applying gypsum board to interior walls. Will shingle roof later if rain lets up. May be getting better at this house-building thing, hammer only went through gypsum board five times. Mrs. Harmeyer says that's okay, she can hang pictures over holes. But Michael says no, we will plaster over them.

Lunch is turkey sandwiches, potato salad, Jell-O, and corn chips. Ate potato salad and Jell-O.

Aw, geez, back to work.

Too tired to write much. Rain let up and I spent afternoon on roof shingling with Lilly, Tina, and Peter Tsu. Only fell off roof once. Landed on Boris, so that was all right. Michael, Lars, and Dr. Gonzales installed the plumbing. Mrs. Harmeyer cried when her toilet flushed for the first time. It was a deeply moving moment.

After dinner—salad, fried chicken, creamed corn, and rolls (only ate salad and rolls)—Michael surprised me by volunteering the two of us to "inventory the tools" in the supply tent.

I wasn't really sure how I felt about that, on account of the whole wet wipe situation. I mean, what if I SMELLED? Made Tina smell me real quick. She said I smelled okay. But who knows if her nostrils are as sensitive as Michael's????

Worried the whole way to supply tent that Michael would try to kiss me, then be repelled by possible b.o.

Except that when we got there, it turned out the supply tent was already occupied . . . by Mr. Wheeton and Mademoiselle Klein, no less!!!!

They made us swear not to tell anyone. We said we wouldn't.

But that is not even the worst part. The worst part is, after they went away, Michael ACTUALLY STARTED INVENTORYING THE TOOLS!!!!!!!!!

There is really only one explanation for this, and that is that I smell so bad, my own boyfriend does not even want to make out with me.

As if this were not bad enough, I felt something crawling up my leg and looked down and saw the world's biggest bug on my calf. I screamed so loud that Lars came bursting in with his gun drawn.

Michael said it was only a centipede.

ONLY A CENTIPEDE? IT TOUCHED MY SKIN!!!!!!!!!

It is much easier to be an environmentalist when you live in the city where there aren't that many bugs, than when you are in the country and are being eaten alive by them. I am not sure I love nature as much as I used to think I did.

Tuesday, March 15, Noon, the dining tent

Worked all morning, still so much left to do, and this is LAST WORK DAY. But still must paint all walls, and trim, too, plus install flooring, etc. Boris dropped a window shutter on his big toe, but Dr. Gonzales said it isn't broken, just dislocated. He manipulated it back into place—I would so never touch Boris's feet. Dr. Gonzales is truly a saint—and buddy-taped it to the toe next to it so it would stay where it is supposed to.

Mrs. Harmeyer has been complaining of heartburn since breakfast, but no one else is feeling sick. Legionnaires' disease ruled out as we have been dining al fresco. Possibly result of two Diet Cokes she downed with her eggs and bacon? Unborn child could be phenylketonuric. Warned Mrs. Harmeyer about dangers of too much aspartame. It is a good thing I have watched so many episodes of *A Baby Story* on the Learning Channel in preparation for the arrival of my new baby brother or sister. I am truly a font of prenatal information.

Tuesday, March 15, 9 p.m., last day of home building

So tired, but truly amazing day, must get it all down before I forget:

Finished building Mr. and Mrs. Harmeyer's house. When we were done, we all stood around and marveled: we had built a three-bedroom, one-bath house in three days, complete with kitchen, dining room, and family room. I mean, it is not a BIG house (only 1,200 square feet, smaller than our loft) and it isn't like the Harmeyers can afford cable or Ikea furniture or anything. But it is a house, not a double wide like Mitchell and Stefano have been living in their whole short lives.

And you know, it didn't look so bad. I mean, we had spackled over the holes I'd made in the gypsum board, so you couldn't even see them. And with the vinyl siding, it looked, I don't know. Like a REAL house.

While we were standing there admiring our handiwork, Mrs. Harmeyer complained that she had a wicked case of heartburn and had anyone else had the potato salad at lunch? I informed Mrs. Harmeyer that, being a vegetarian, I had eaten nothing but potato salad for lunch, as it had been the only non-meat dish available, and that I felt fine. Then I opened my diary to the entry I wrote earlier today and showed Mrs. Harmeyer that she had complained of indigestion after breakfast, as well. Was it possible, I asked, that she wasn't having heartburn at all, but contractions? The two have occasionally been confused, even by experienced mothers, at least according to *A Baby Story*.

Then Mrs. Harmeyer got all excited and yelled, "Oh, my God! Todd, git the pickup!"

So Mr. and Mrs. Harmeyer sped off for the hospital, leaving us in charge of Mitchell and Stefano. Dr. Gonzales was way impressed by what he called my powers of observation. Not everybody, he said, would have kept such a detailed record of another person's complaints about their gastritis.

I told Dr. Gonzales that it was no big deal, that I write down everything, really. Then he said the funniest thing. He said: "That's quite a skill."

Wow! It almost made me think maybe being able to write isn't such a bad talent, after all! I mean, it isn't as cool as being able to use a nail gun, and all. But hey, it might not be *totally* useless.

Then Dr. Gonzales turned to Michael and said, "We're out of hot-dog buns for the celebration barbecue tonight. If I stay here with Mitchell and Stefano, do you think you could go into town and pick some up?" And he handed Michael the keys to his Dodge Chevy!

And it turns out Michael can drive! He has a driver's license and everything! He learned two summers ago at his parents' country house in Albany.

There are very few boys who live in Manhattan who

know how to drive, on account of hardly anyone owning a car in New York City.

So Michael said, "Sure, Dr. Gonzales."

For a minute I thought a Spring Break miracle had occurred . . . you know, that Michael and I would be alone, in a motor vehicle, miles from anybody else, and would finally get a chance to feel our two hearts beat as one. . . .

That is, if I could get cleaned up fast enough.

But I needn't have worried. Because no sooner did Michael get those keys in his hands than we were descended upon by the rest of our group, who all demanded to join us. I tried not to look too depressed as Lars, Lilly, Boris, Tina, and Peter Tsu piled into the truck with us. Their enthusiasm *was* a little bit infectious, I have to admit.

Town was a big disappointment, though. I'd forgotten that Mrs. Harmeyer had said there was nothing to do in it. There is not even a single Chinese restaurant where you can go for cold sesame noodles. We went to the grocery store and got the hot-dog buns, and Lilly was all, "Finally, I can get a bagel!" But they didn't even have any, not even the Lender's kind in a bag.

So then we were all kind of depressed on account of the no-bagel-and-no-cold-sesame-noodle thing. But when we got back in the truck, Michael went, "Well, there's one thing West Virginia has that Manhattan doesn't," and he started driving.

I thought Michael was talking about the Mothman, you know, from that movie, and I couldn't think what was so great about that because all the Mothman does is call people on the phone and say in a scary voice, "Stay away from the chemical plant!" which isn't really useful information to anyone.

But it turns out Michael wasn't talking about the Mothman. He was talking about Dairy Queen! Yes! It turns out there was a Dairy Queen right outside Hominy Knob! There are no Dairy Queens in Manhattan, except for a gross one nobody but tourists ever goes to in Penn Station.

We were so excited, we piled out of the truck and rushed up to the girl in the window. Everybody got something different. Lars got a cherry slush. Lilly got a peanut buster parfait. Boris got a Heath Bar bite blizzard. Peter Tsu got a Coke slush. Tina got low-cal yogurt on account of the fact that Peter Tsu was looking. Michael got an Oreo cookie blizzard. I got a chocolate-dipped vanilla soft serve.

And it was SO good! After all our hard work, and the sleeping in tents and the Port-O-Lets and the wet wipes and slathering on cherry ChapStick for nothing and finding out that I actually have a useful talent after all, that chocolate-dipped vanilla cone was really the most delicious thing I had ever eaten in my whole life.

We were all enjoying our ice cream, leaning against

the side of the Dodge Chevy in the soft pre-spring sun-
shine, when a large black limo slithered into the Dairy
Queen parking lot. I swear I nearly dropped my vanilla
cone as the chauffeur came around to open the rear
passenger door, and out popped—

"Grandmère!" I cried, barely able to believe my
eyes.

"Amelia," Grandmère said, looking around in dis-
taste. She was dressed in a big feathered purple velvet
coat, with Rommel in one arm and a purse in the other.
All the residents of Hominy Knob who happened to be
in the vicinity could not take their eyes off her. "You're
looking . . . fit."

"Grandmère," I said. "What are you *doing* here? I
thought you were going to Palm Springs."

"I did go there. I thought I would stop by to see you
on my way home. I've been to your, er, work site."

"Really?" I was still shocked to see Grandmère in
Hominy Knob. "Did you see the house we built?"

"I did," Grandmère said. "I must admit, when you
told me this is what you wanted to do with your Spring
Break, I thought you were mad. But I met Dr.
Gonzales, and he seems like a very nice man. And your
house is . . . adequate. That is not, however, why I am
here. I've taken rooms at the Hampton Inn—sadly,
the finest quarters I was able to procure. I thought
perhaps you all might like to come back with me and
shower before your little celebration dinner, to which

Dr. Gonzales has very kindly invited me. I understand the bathing conditions at the camp are on the primitive side, and all of you have a very long bus ride ahead of you tomorrow."

We piled back into the truck without another word. Take a shower? No one needed to ask us twice. The thought that we might, at long last, be able to scrape four days of sweat and dew from our bodies was even better than ice cream—even better, I must admit, than the prospect of uninterrupted kissing.

So we all followed Grandmère's limo to the motel, where she'd taken seven rooms for herself and Rommel, her bodyguards, her personal maid, her assistant, her chauffeur, and her clothes. Everybody got to fully submerge themselves under nice hot water and use some clean towels for a change. I myself borrowed some of Grandmère's Chanel No. 5 and fully spritzed my clothes with it. Bliss!!!! Now there was NO WAY my boyfriend would be able to resist me.

Although when I presented myself to him, in all of my squeaky-clean glory, by the ice machine in the Hampton Inn hallway, any attempt Michael might have made to kiss me was cruelly thwarted by Grandmère's maid, who came strolling by with Rommel on a leash, because it was time for "walkies."

After we had all finished washing away the sawdust and dew, we politely thanked Grandmère and said we had to be going back to camp in order to deliver the hot-dog buns. When we got there, we found out that Mrs. Harmeyer had given birth to a healthy six-pound-five-ounce baby girl. But what REALLY blew me away was when Dr. Gonzales said, "And, Mia, the Harmeyers said to tell you that they named her after you."

"Really?" I was flattered. "They named their baby Mia?"

Dr. Gonzales looked uncomfortable. "Uh," he said. "Not exactly. They named her Princess."

Princess Harmeyer. Oh, well. It's still nice to know I have left my mark on Hominy Knob. Sort of.

After the celebration dinner—which was really nice; they seemed to have run out of corn products—Dr. Gonzales built a campfire and we roasted marshmallows. Michael got out his guitar and we all sang that "Kum ba ya" song, the one that makes me feel like crying every time I hear it.

Then to show our West Virginia hosts some New York City "flava," Lilly, and Tina, and I sang our version of Destiny's Child's "Survivor," which we do very well (Lilly even let me be Beyoncé for a change). Grandmère clapped like crazy, even though Lars laughed so hard that he almost choked on a s'more and Mrs. Hill had to smack him on the back.

Then the host families sang a West Virginia song that was very sad, about a girl who may have been born poor white trash, but Fancy was her name. It was all about how Fancy used her talents to get ahead in life. She never complained about having the WRONG KIND of talent, she just used what God gave her. That, I realized, is what *I* need to start doing: stop wishing for better talents, and just learn to use the one I have to the best of my ability.

I sighed pretty hard when I thought of this, and Michael must have thought I was sad or something, since he put his arm around me. YES!!!!!!!!! The guy was finally starting to come around.

Then we had some nice passionate moments making out near his tent while he was supposed to be putting his guitar away.

All I can say is . . . thank you. THANK YOU, GRANDMÈRE!!!! Because without her and the use of her shower, Michael and I might never have developed the very great appreciation for the theology of the hammer that we have right now.

I am home!!!!!!!!! AT LAST!!!!!!!!!!

The bus ride back from West Virginia was SO much better than the bus ride there. For one thing, Principal Gupta made sure Boris was good and dosed with Dramamine before she let him anywhere near the parking lot. And then everybody was so tired, they all fell asleep before we even got onto Highway 64.

When the bus finally pulled up in front of Albert Einstein High School and everyone started piling off to collect their bags from Charlie, there was a lot of hugging and "See you Monday" going on from people who before the trip hadn't been friends. Like between us and Peter Tsu.

The funniest part was, Dr. Gonzales came up to me, looking all embarrassed and went, "Princess Mia, please tell your grandmother that I enjoyed meeting her very much. She is truly a dynamic woman."

Whoa. Looks like I'm not the only Renaldo who turns out to have a secret talent.

I am so happy to be home, I ran around kissing everything I'd missed, including Fat Louie, the mattress on my bed, my bathtub, the refrigerator, and the TV.

But most of all I kissed my mom, and told her that even though West Virginia is all right and everything, it is really true what Dorothy says in *The Wizard of Oz*, about there being no place like home.

"Even if you're on Spring Break?" my mom wanted to know.

"Even if you're on Spring Break," I said.

"Even if you're a princess?" my mom asked.

"*Especially* if you're a princess," I said.

And then I picked up the phone and called Number One Noodle Son and ordered us all some cold sesame noodles for dinner.

Turn the page for an excerpt from

The Princess Diaries, Volume V:
Princess in Pink!

THE ATOM

The Official Student-Run Newspaper of Albert Einstein High School

Take Pride in the AEHS Lions

Week of May 5   *Volume 456/Issue 27*

Science Fair Winners Announced

by Rafael Menendez

Science students entered 21 projects in the Albert Einstein High School Science Fair. Several projects advanced to the New York City regional competition, which will be held next month. Senior Judith Gershner received the grand prize for slicing a human genome. Earning special honors were senior Michael Moscovitz for his computer program modeling the death of a dwarf star, and freshman Kenneth Showalter for his experiments in gender transfiguration in newts.

Lacrosse Teams Win

by Ai-Lin Hong

Both the varsity and junior varsity lacrosse teams beat their competitors this past weekend. Senior Josh Richter led the varsity team to a stunning defeat of the Dwight School 7–6 in overtime. The JV team defeated Dwight by a score of 8–0. The exciting games were marred by a peculiarly aggressive Central Park squirrel that continuously darted out onto the field. Eventually it was chased away by Principal Gupta.

AEHS's Princess Spends Spring Break Building Homes for Appalachian Poor

by Melanie Greenbaum

Spring break was a working holiday for AEHS freshman Mia Thermopolis. Mia, who, it was revealed last fall is actually the sole heir to the throne of the principality of Genovia, spent her five-day vacation helping build homes for Housing for the Hopeful. Said the princess of her sojourn into the foothills of the Smokey Mountains, building two-bedroom homes for the underprivileged: "It was okay. Except for the whole no bathroom thing. And the part where I kept hitting myself in the thumb with my hammer."

Senior Week
by Josh Richter,
senior class president

The week of May 5–May 10 is Senior Week. This is the time to honor this year's AEHS graduating class, who has worked so hard to show you leadership throughout the year. The Senior Week Events Calendar goes like this:

Mon:
Senior Awards Banquet

Tues:
Senior Sports Banquet

Wed:
Senior Debate

Thurs:
Senior Skit Nite

Fri:
Senior Skip Day

Sat:
Senior Prom

A Note From Your Principal:

Senior Skip Day is not an event sanctioned by school administration. All students are required to attend classes Friday, May 9. In addition, the request made by certain members of the freshman class to lift the sanction against underclassmen attending the prom unless invited by an upperclassman is denied.

Notice to All Students:

It has come to the attention of the administration that many pupils do not seem to

2

know the proper words to the AEHS school song. They are as follows:

Einstein Lions, we're for you
Come on, be bold, come on,
be bold, come on, be bold
Einstein Lions, we're for you
Blue and gold, blue
and gold, blue and gold
Einstein Lions, we're for you
We've got a team no one
else can ever tame
Einstein Lions, we're for you
Let's win this game!

Please note that at this year's graduation ceremony, any student caught singing alternative (particularly explicit and/or suggestive) words to the AEHS school song will be removed from the premises. Complaints that the AEHS school song is too militaristic must be submitted in writing to the AEHS administrative office, not scrawled on bathroom door stalls or discussed on any student's public access television program.

Letters to the Editor:

To Whom it May Concern:
Melanie Greenbaum's article in last week's issue of the *Atom* on the strides the women's movement has made in the past three decades was laughably facile. Sexism is still alive and well, not only around the world, but in our own country. In Utah, for instance, polygamous marriages involving brides as young as 11 years of age are thriving, practiced by fundamentalist Mormons who continue to live by traditions their ancestors brought west in the mid-1800s. The number of people in polygamous families in Utah is estimated by human rights groups at perhaps as many as 50,000, despite the fact that polygamy is not tolerated by the mainstream Mormon church, and the enactment of tough penalties in the case of underage brides that can sentence a polygamous husband or church leader arranging

such a marriage to up to 15 years in prison.

I am not telling other cultures how to live, or anything. I am just saying take off the rose-colored glasses, Ms. Greenbaum, and write an article about some of the real problems that affect half the population of this planet. The staff of the *Atom* might well consider giving some of their other writers a chance to report on these issues, instead of relegating them to the cafeteria beat.
—Lilly Moscovitz

Take out your own personal ad! Available to AEHS students at 50 cents/line

4

AEHS Food Court Menu
compiled by Mia Thermopolis

Mon. Potato Bar, Fr. Bread Pizza, Fish Fingers,
Meatball Sub, Spicy Chix

Tues. Soup & Sand, Chicken Patty, Tuna in Pita,
Indiv. Pizza, Nachos Deluxe

Wed. Taco Salad Bar, Burrito, Corndog/Pickle, Deli Bar,
Italian Beef

Thurs. Asian Bar, Chicken Parm, Corn/FF Pasta Bar,
Fish Stix

Fri. Bean Bar, Grilled Cheese, Curley Fries,
Buffalo Bites, Soft Pretzel

Will Michael ask Mia to the prom?
Will Josh Richter ever learn the words
to the AEHS school song?*
Is Lilly *really* Boris's true love?
And will Mia ever move up from covering
the school paper's cafeteria beat?

Find out in
The Princess Diaries, Volume V:
Princess in Pink

*We may never know the answer to that one.

READ ALL THE BOOKS ABOUT MIA:

The Princess Diaries

VOL. II: Princess in the Spotlight

VOL. III: Princess in Love

VOL. IV: Princess in Waiting

VOL. IV ½: Project Princess

VOL. V: Princess in Pink

VOL. VI: Princess in Training

PRINCESS DIARIES BOOKS

The Princess Present

Princess Lessons

Perfect Princess